THISTLE

by Walter Wangerin, Jr.

pictures by Marcia Sewall

Harper & Row, Publishers

Thistle
Text copyright © 1983 by Walter M. Wangerin, Jr.
Illustrations copyright © 1983 by Marcia Sewall
For information address
Harper & Row, Publishers, Inc., 10 East 53rd Street,
New York, N.Y. 10022. Published simultaneously in
Canada by Fitzhenry & Whiteside Limited, Toronto.

Library of Congress Cataloging in Publication Data
Wangerin, Walter.
    Thistle.

    Summary: Plain Thistle can only cry as one by one
her family is eaten by the potato monster Pudge, but
her gentle bargain with a witch saves them all.
    [1. Monsters—Fiction.   2. Witches—Fiction]
I. Sewall, Marcia, ill.   II. Title.
PZ7.W1814Th 1983   [E]   82-47717
ISBN 0-06-026351-2
ISBN 0-06-026352-0 (lib. bdg.)

First Edition
Designed by Al Cetta
1 2 3 4 5 6 7 8 9 10

For my children,
whose tears I know too well,
whose laughter is as dazzling
as an answered prayer.

ONCE UPON A TIME there lived a man and his wife in a potato house. It was called the potato house not because it was made of potatoes, but because that is what the good man did. That was his work. He grew potatoes.

All day long and every day from the cold to the cold of the year, the good man labored in his field, tilling and planting, weeding and growing, digging and storing potatoes. Just once a day he would come home, and then it was to eat. "Hungry!" he would cry, flinging open the door exactly at noon. "I am hungry! And, good wife, I mean to eat! Where is my dinner?"

One thing only troubled their lives: they had no children, though they wished with all their hearts for sons and daughters. The man in his field and the woman at home were lonely.

But this was a problem soon solved.

They had a son. He was tall, and he carried himself as straight as any tree. He was blessed with fine good looks, a slender trunk, and eyes as green as mystery. Therefore they called him Pine, and they were glad that the family had grown by one.

In time they had another son. This lad was strong. His arm was as hard as the branch of a tree, his back all barky with muscle, and his thigh a-ripple with muscles as quick as triggers. So they called him Oak, and they laughed for joy that the family had grown by two.

Then the Lord thought to bless them with a daughter, and the man and his wife each held their breath when they saw how beautiful she was. Her skin was so petaled and pale, the blush on her cheek so red and rare, that the wind itself would sigh when

kissing her. They called her Rose, and they wept sweetly to think that the family had grown by three.

Finally there was born to them a fourth child, unlike the other three. Short she was, stumpy, a little too chubby, too low in the waist, her fingers both clumsy and thick. But they loved her perhaps the most, because she needed them the most. And they were an honest couple, the man and his wife, so they named her Thistle, and they protected the child as best they could.

When Pine grew proud and called her "Short" from his green and handsome height; when Oak, impatient, pushed her aside and told her she was too fat; when Rose would smile as cold as ice, and Thistle would cry in her hands, then the man and the woman would speak to them. "She is your sister. She is our daughter and the youngest of us all," they said. "She should not cry. The Lord loves the little, and the good will walk in the ways of the Lord. Pine, she should not cry. Oak and Rose, she shouldn't be made to cry, no, not so much as a tear."

And so it went for many years. The good man labored in the field, coming home at noon to stand in the doorway and shout: "Hungry! I am hungry! And, good wife, I mean to eat! Where is my dinner?"

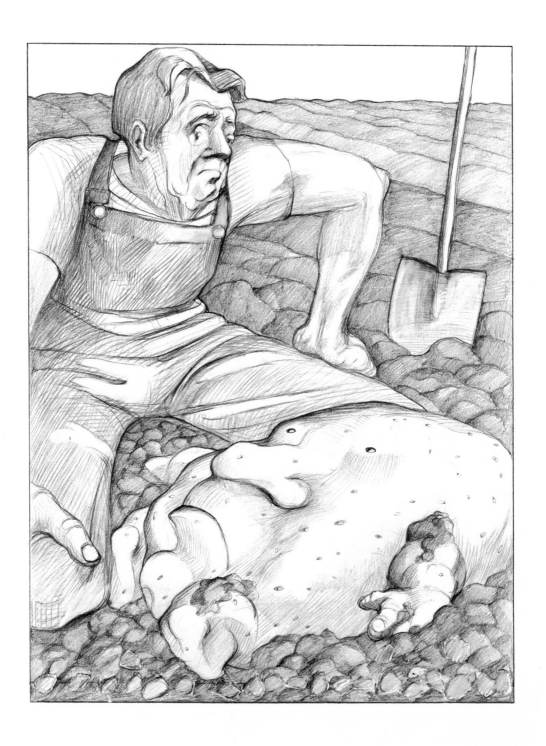

But one morning the good man struck a potato like none he had ever seen before. It was enormous. His shovel bit a piece of its skin, and it seemed to moan, so the man knelt down and with his fingers dug the dirt away. He uncovered a tuber rough and soft and twice his size. It had two stubby lumps at the sides of it, and two at the bottom, and a thousand eyes all over—as any potato should have, but these were large, large.

Suddenly, one of the eyes opened up and stared straight at him. Now, this was a wonder, so he stopped digging and considered what it meant to be looked at by a potato.

Then the four lumps trembled and jerked. They began to move like arms and legs, kicking the dirt and climbing. The potato sat up. Other eyes popped open. The good man jumped backward, perfectly astonished, unable to speak a word. But this potato could do what the man could not.

In a voice both mashed and mealy, thick and horrible, it roared: "My name is Pudge! And I am hungry!" A thousand eyes now glared at one good man, and the voice roared on. "Good man, I mean to eat, and here is my dinner before me. I will eat you!"

And that, in a twinkling, is what Pudge did. Pudge ate the good man, shoes, shovel, and all.

Now up on bumpish legs, Pudge walked to the good man's house, arriving just at noon. Pudge did not knock, but flung wide the door and stamped a squashy foot and roared, "My name is Pudge! And I am hungry!"

The good woman and four children stared at a thousand eyes staring back at them. Who could utter a word at such a meeting? Pudge could.

"Hungry!" thundered Pudge. "I am hungry! And, good woman, since I mean to eat, I will eat you."

Which is what Pudge did, swallowed the woman and left.

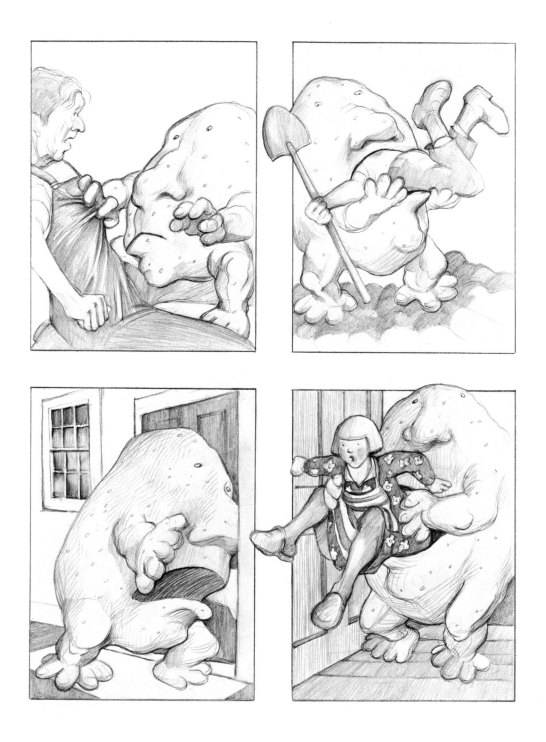

So THERE stood Pine perpendicular, and Oak muscle-bound, and Rose in a pretty faint, and Thistle—four children shocked and alone.

"What are we going to do?" they asked one another, drooping.

Thistle cried.

"Shoosh, Thistle," they said to the youngest of all. "Can you do nothing but cry? No, nothing but cry," they said.

Then Pine straightened himself. "Well, I am the oldest," he said, lifting his nose to an inspiring height. "I am also the tallest and the most handsome. Therefore it is my job to save us. I will go out into the wide world and find some way to fight the ugly Pudge, and we will be right after all."

So the others patted him on the back and praised him and wished him farewell, glad to have such an older brother. And, while Thistle wept in worry on account of him, he went away.

For a long time Pine walked the roads and traveled the highways and chanced the tangled woods of the wide world. High and low he sought some weapon by which he might fight Pudge, some magical something, if magic were to be found. But he found nothing.

Finally, he saw a witch sitting on a stump.

She was truly hideous. Her nose stuck out ten inches from her face, all covered with warts. Her chin stuck out ten inches from her throat, all covered with drool. And the tips of them touched like the

claws of a crab, that opened and shut when she talked. So hunched was she, that her knees came up above her ears. And she had but three gray hairs upon her head.

Instantly Pine decided that there could be no good in talking to one so miserable and short. He began to pass her by.

But she spoke.

"Handsome lad, where be thee going?" croaked the witch, her nose and her chin a-pinching the air.

"Oh, madam, no business of yours," said Pine, his nose held higher than ever.

"Ah," croaked the witch, staring up at the tall fellow from between her knees. "Ah," she nodded knowingly. "Aha, but I can read the green of thine eye. 'Tis a weapon thou seekest, right? For 'twas a Pudge did gobble down thy father first and then thy mother. And now, Green Eyes, thou hast taken upon thee to fight a Pudge thyself. Right? Right?"

Pine paused before such knowledge. Pine looked down at her.

"Well, lad," she croaked, "I can lend thee such a weapon as will make a monster's tummy ache."

Now that was of interest to Pine, so he spoke to her, though carelessly.

"What can shortness give a tall fellow like me?" he asked.

"Whisht! Whisht! Not so quickly!" croaked the witch. "We'll make a trade of it. Before I give thee what thou needest, let me give a thing to satisfy meself—"

"And what," said Pine, "can satisfy a crone so old as you?"

"Kisses, lad!" quoth the witch. "A hundred kisses from these old and lonely lips! 'Tis a nose and a chin, you see, have stopped me sweetest kissing, and never may I kiss except some child be willing to receive it. Green Eyes," whispered the witch so humbly, "let me but kiss thee, lad."

Well, Pine did not want kisses from between a warty nose and a slippery chin. He was much too tall and far too handsome for that. So he drew himself up to a splendid height and said, "I'll take what weapons you may have to offer. But as for kisses, madam, keep them. I want none of those."

Down went the witch's head at that reply, down deeper between her knees. Her eyes grew slittier than the edges of knives, for she was very angry. But she smiled a sort of smile, and she sang softly:

"Then take thee, lad, what is thy due,
 A clutch of weapons fit for you:
 No bow nor blade nor studded boots.
 No need for these—*thou shalt have roots*."

Roots, thought Pine. Good! Anything given to one as handsome as he was must surely be worthy and good, fine weapons for fighting Pudge.

Home went Pine at high speed. Nobly he took up his place facing the door. Taller and prouder than ever was he, and his eyes more green than the whirling leaves of the forest, since he was about to fight the most important fight of all.

His brother and sisters stepped backward, silently.

Precisely at noon the door flew open, and there stood Pudge, two lumpish arms, two thickish legs, and a thousand eyes a-blazing.

"My name is Pudge!" Pudge roared. Pine threw back his head. "Hungry! I am hungry!" Pudge roared. Pine raised his arms to a point above his head, preparing to learn what sort of weapons roots were, preparing to attack. "And you, you toothpick," Pudge thundered at Pine, "since I mean to eat, I will eat you!"

Now Pine tried to move—but he couldn't take a step. He was absolutely fixed to the floor. By roots! *Roots!*

And Pudge rolled forward, and Pudge ate him up and left.

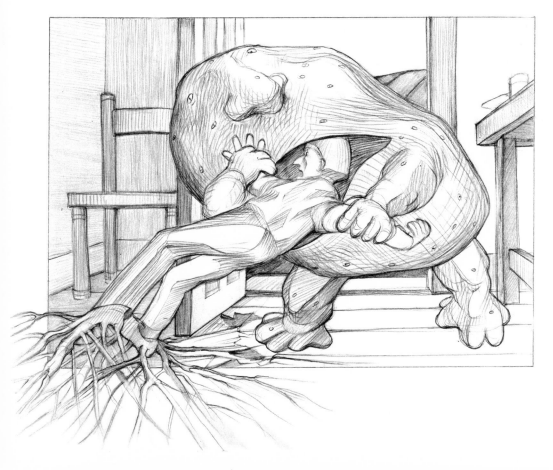

SIX WERE FOUR, for the loss of two parents. Then four were three. And now one of the three was weeping in her hands.

"Shoosh, Thistle," they said to her. "Can you do nothing but cry? No, nothing but cry," they said.

But Oak never cried. Oak was sturdy, and he said so.

"I am the strongest," he said, flexing all his muscles. "Few words, that's me. By action both quick and powerful, that's how I go. So I'm gone, my sisters, to find the weapon to save us!"

And Oak was gone, leaving one in the potato house who wept for him.

As it happened, Oak followed the same path that Pine had taken. Soon, then, he came to the witch on her stump, dripping drops of drool from the tip of her nose to the tip of her chin.

"Strong swain!" she croaked. "Where be thee traveling?"

"To war," he snapped.

"Ah." The witch slid her eyes to the left and the right. "Is the world at war and I knew it not?"

"Pish, elder! What could you know on your stump?" said Oak. "I go to gain a victory. To slice the potato named Pudge. To save my sisters. I lack but the weapon to do it."

"Weapons, weapons, the world wants weapons," sighed the witch, "whereas I sit here full of the cunningest weapons for cutting potatoes to bits."

"Well, then," Oak demanded, snapping his fingers, "give them to one who can use them, elder. Quickly, and I'll be gone."

The witch nodded as slowly as the sea. "Time, swain, time," she croaked. "There be time enough for two to come to terms. The weapons thou shalt surely have, if first I may give thee something of my own liking, though no use to thee—"

"Whatever!" Oak said, stamping a foot.

"Ah, he saith *whatever*," drawled the witch. "'Tis a generous answer, that—"

"Terms, elder!" Oak shouted. "Tell me your terms and I'll go!"

Now the witch looked directly at Oak with a glittering eye. "Let me," she croaked, "let me kiss thee."

Oak frowned. He folded his arms across his chest. He gave a three-second glance to the ancient woman crouched like a toad upon her stump, and then he said, "Pish." He snapped his fingers. "Keep your kisses," he commanded. "Give me weapons. I am no lover, but a fighter!"

Again, the witch's eyes grew sharper than knives. And anger brought her knees together above her head. But she smiled a thin smile and whispered, "Roots," as though it were a lover's word after all.

> "Snakes and serpents, adders, newts
>   For all thy muscles substitutes!
>   I'll send thee, swain,
>   To home again
>   With right reward: *Thou shalt have roots*."

"Gibberish," mumbled Oak, and he ran back to the potato house where he pushed his sisters out of the way and stood foursquare before the door, waiting for Pudge and certain that roots had something to do with strength.

They did. Strongly they held him to the floor, so that he could neither fight nor run; and at noon the roaring Pudge consumed him, too.

Six WERE FOUR, then four were three. Now two alone were left, and one of these was crying.

"Shoosh, shoosh, Thistle," said Rose. "Can you do nothing but cry? No, nothing but cry."

But Rose had no mind to comfort her sister; her mind was all full of her own private plans. She touched the blush on her left cheek and thought, Things of beauty last forever. She touched the blush on her right cheek and thought, Because beauty can turn the foe against himself! "Thistle," she said aloud, "no need to stir yourself. I'll be back in a bit." And she was gone, and Thistle was alone.

Rose, like her brothers before her, met the witch and was shocked to find so much ugliness in one spare body.

And as the witch had asked the brothers, so she asked the sister whither she was going. But Rose would answer not a word. Instead, she stared ahead with icy eyes, hoping that soon the witch would see the difference between the two of them and be properly ashamed.

But the witch knew no shame. Bluntly she croaked the terms of her trade: "An exchange, my pretty. Weapons for kisses. Let me kiss thee, and then I shall dress thee in weapons."

Rose was not surprised by this request. The rocks and stones themselves would kiss her, if they had the lips, and if she gave permission.

"Those," she said with a toss of her head, "who someday kiss me shall be worthy of the opportunity. That's one or two, just one or two in all the world. And you," she said to the witch, "are not among them."

The witch nodded and nodded and nodded as though this were a pretty saying, worth remembering. So low had her head descended, that her chin was scratching the ground. So slitty were her eyes, that they might have cut. And so softly did she whisper, that Rose could hardly hear the spell:

> "To her who thinks she tallies best
> I'll give what I gave all the rest;
> What suited theirs, my pretty, suits
> Thine heart as well: *Thou shalt have roots.*"

Rose neither blinked nor blanched. She merely nodded. "My brothers were fools who never knew what to do with your gift," she said. "But I'm no fool. Roots is it? Well, I'll take your evil and make it my good."

The witch closed her eyes with a smile as bleak as any winter.

But Rose went lightly home, told Thistle to keep to her place, and turned to wait for Pudge.

So Pudge appeared, roaring a hunger and roaring the food that could fill it. "Sugar!" Pudge thundered, aiming a thousand droopy eyes at Rose. "I've a tooth for sugar, and so I will eat you!"

But Rose showed no fear. She smiled most sweetly upon the potato. Around one stubby arm she tangled a root. With roots she caressed the rotten hide. And she nuzzled Pudge as though she were in love.

Thistle screamed.

Rose turned.

"Shoosh!" she hissed, stamping her foot. And in that instant Pudge bellowed, "DESSERT!" and swallowed the Rose down whole.

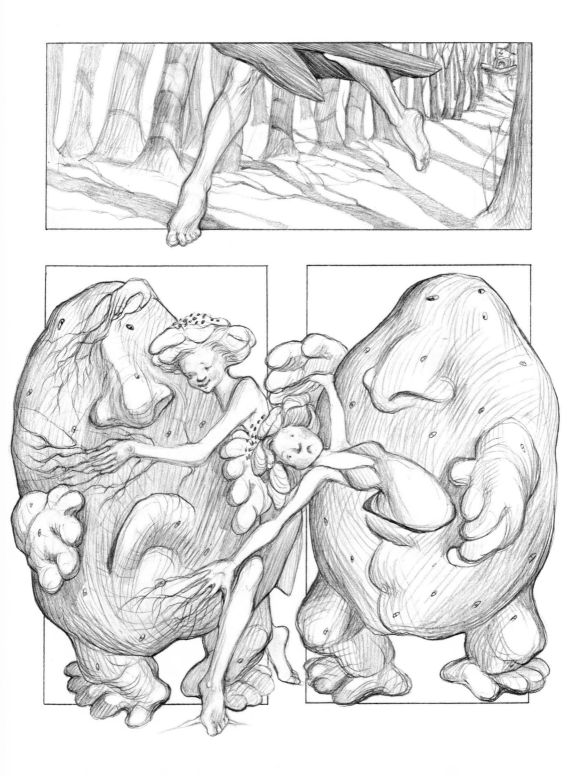

Six WERE FOUR, and four but two, and two no more than one. Poor Thistle, poor youngest of them all, left all alone in the potato house.

"Can you do nothing but cry?" she said to herself. "No, nothing but cry." she said. The tears rained down. The sobbing shook her. And the sighs just echoed in an empty house.

"I wish I were tall," she wept. But she was short.

"I wish I were strong." But she was weak.

"Dear God, I wish I were beautiful." But she was a plain sort, with nothing of value and nothing to

use in the fight against Pudge, nothing, no, nothing but tears.

Poor Thistle. She stumbled from the house and into the world, meaning to go nowhere, for she knew nowhere to go. All the world was a lonely place. All the sky was gray, and all the ground gone stony, and all the cockleburs clutched at her as she passed by. And the forest did not love her.

Poor Thistle. She walked and cried and cried and named her family one by one, out loud, with love and sorrow. But when she had named the last of them, a voice croaked, "I am acquainted with three of these."

Thistle rubbed her eyes. There, on a stump, sat a witch, as old as stone and ugly.

"You knew them?" asked the girl.

"Very well," croaked the witch; and Thistle accepted her words as kindness, since anyone who knew her brothers and sister must be kind. "I met them each by each," croaked the bunch-backed witch, "and each by each I sent them home again."

"Oh, Mother!" Thistle burst into fresh tears. "What can I do? Pudge has eaten all the height and strength and beauty of the world. What is left? What is left?"

"Little and nothing," quoth the witch, "save that I may give thee something worth nothing at all to thee, except it pleases me to give it. Wilt thou have it?"

"Mother, please yourself," wept Thistle.

"Ai!" cried the witch, half rising from her crouch. "And dost not ask, first, what I mean to give thee?"

Thistle, sobbing, shook her head.

"Child, let me kiss thee," breathed the witch.

And Thistle said simply, "Kiss me."

So then the witch slid down from her stump and hobbled to Thistle and kissed her. Not once, but a thousand times she kissed her. Every tear poor Thistle shed, the witch kissed it.

And then this is what happened.

Each tear that was kissed turned into a thorn. Soon Thistle was covered by tiny thorns. And the witch—she whispered, "Done!

"Cap-a-pie and foot to brow,
One child is weaponed now."

She hobbled back to her stump. And just before she entered it and disappeared, she said in a musical voice, "Child, go home again. Wait thee there for Pudge, then we shall see what we shall see—"

Thistle. Ah, Thistle. Dear Thistle went home again.

In the same place where Pine stood tall, where Oak had muscled his defense and Rose had wilted in her beauty, there Thistle sat down. No hope was in her. She simply sat and waited.

BOOM! The door flew open. Pudge was huge. Pudge was bloat, swollen with all of her family.

"My name is Pudge!" Pudge thundered, louder than ever before. "And yours is porridge. Hungry! I am still hungry!" the lubber roared. "And now I will eat you!"

Forward Pudge thumped on stubby legs, and Thistle bowed her head. A thousand eyes rolled all around her. A mouth gaped wide above her, and Thistle was swallowed with one gulp, all the way down to the stomach.

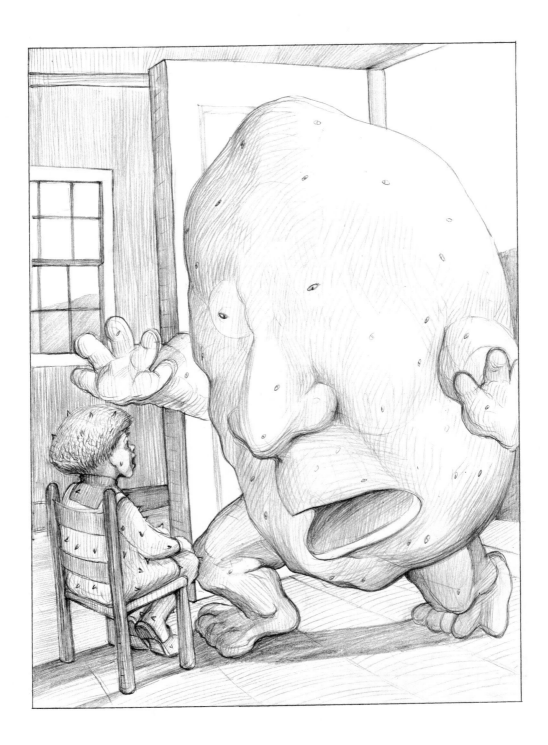

But this time Pudge did not go away.

The thousand eyes began to blink furiously and to shed tears. The thick arms beat their sides. The fat mouth opened in a terrible groan, for the thorns were stinging Pudge! Thistle's little thorns were sticking in the gullet and the guts of the great potato—burning!

"WHAT DID I EAT?" Pudge bellowed, falling to the floor and rolling about in pain. "WHAT DID I EAT? AND WHAT IS EATING ME?"

The pain swelled larger and larger inside, till Pudge did burst at the middle, spewing mashed potato all over the house.

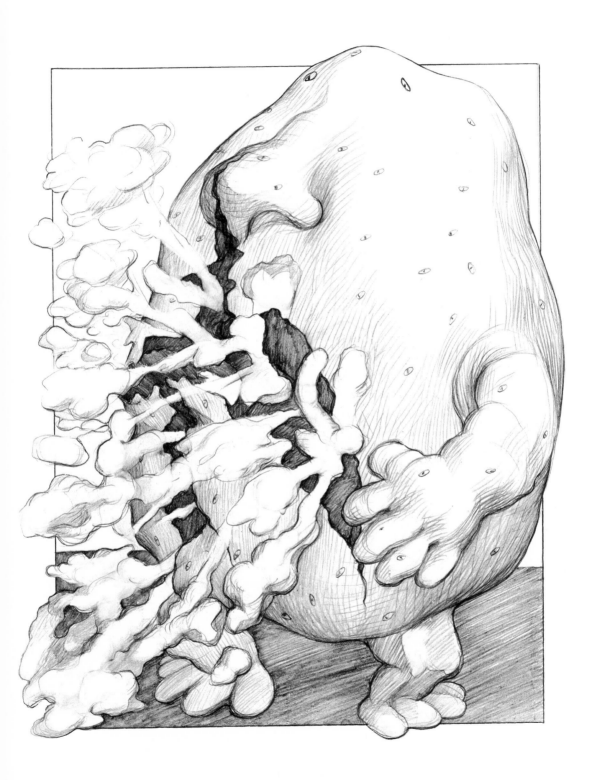

And out of the hole came Thistle! And next came Rose and Oak and Pine, alive and happy and well. And then the good man and his wife stepped out of the hole together; and who was it they looked for? Why, for Thistle.

What a hugging was in the potato house that day. The family threw arms around each other, and danced, and laughed, and cried; and no one said

"No" to the tears anymore, but everyone wept them
together. For by her crying Thistle had brought
them back to life, and by her loving they were
saved.

The good man and his good wife, they kissed
their Thistle specially.

And Pudge—Pudge was made into soup.